ALASKApacas
Furbanks, Moorage & Homer

Written by **Helen von Ammon**
Illustrations by **Erin Mauterer**

Doodlebug Books   SAN FRANCISCO

Text ©2001 by Helen von Ammon / Illustrations ©2001 by Erin Mauterer

Published by
Doodlebug Books / von Ammon Studios
850 Powell St. #500
San Francisco, CA 94108-2040 USA

Distributed by
Todd Communications
203 W. 15th Ave. Suite 102
Anchorage, Alaska 99501
Tel. (907) 274-8633   Fax (907) 276-6858
e-mail: sales@toddcom.com

Illustrations by Erin Mauterer, Bluewater Advertising & Design, Ocean, New Jersey
Book design by Diane O'Neill, Todd Communications, Anchorage, Alaska
Printed in Korea on recycled paper.

CIP 00-093442
ISBN 0-9647756-9-7

Acknowledgment

My profound thanks to Carolyn and Gordon Anderson of Washington and Janet and Jim Faiks of Alaska. Unstintingly you shared with me your alpacas, experience, knowledge and made this book possible.

To my friend Kevin Crisp – your incredible patience and wizardry rescued me from countless computer crises. I am deeply grateful. Without your help and sense of humor I would have reverted to pen and yellow lined pad.

CHAPTER 1

Max and Reggie nudged Lynn Halybut's waist with their massive heads. The French Briard brothers from the same puppy litter had decided it was past their breakfast time. Pony tails of shaggy, wheat-colored fur covered their black, shiny eyes. But they could see very well and never missed a thing. Lynn filled their food dishes, "Eat quickly, big guys. It's such a beautiful day I'm sorry I must banish you to pens inside the barn."

A strange truck pulled into the ALASKApacas Ranch driveway and parked near fenced pastures. Abandoning their breakfast, temporarily, they barked fiercely, rushing to check out the intruder. Lynn glanced out the window, "Thank you, boys, but we don't need your help just now. But we DO need Homer. Is that boy still sleeping?!"

Looking out over the large pasture, Homer smiled. The sun disappeared beyond distant mountains, replaced by millions of stars. Three female alpacas, their bellies big and barrel-shaped, enjoyed this separate maternity pasture. They nibbled grass, vividly green from daily spring rain. Rolling over and over in bare, brown dirt was such fun. Clouds of dust swirled, clinging to their furry bodies. Not a pretty sight! Their thick woolly coats, softer than the finest human hair, became soiled and chocolate colored. They always rolled in the same hole and it grew bigger and deeper every year. Rollicking and rolling through fragrant wild camomile plants refreshed their coats a little. 'Paca folks say they roll to keep away bugs. Alpacas think it's fun to "bug" the person who grooms them, usually Homer.

Homer stood atop a small hill, raised his arms – like an orchestra maestro. Alpacas gathered 'round him, expectantly hoping for grain treats. Green-brown alpaca chow would also be acceptable. Speaking quietly, he smiled, raising his arms. They gave him their full attention. "Ladies, you have enjoyed this maternity pasture for eleven months. **Now it is TIME!** Who's going to be first?"

Crias are usually born as the mother stands. But Junebug, pushy and independent as always, kushed on the soft, clean grass, exclaiming, "I'm first!" First her front legs bent under, then back legs, her short tail raised high. Almost at once a tiny, shiny wet nose appeared under her uplifted tail. Two salmon colored, perfect two-toed hoofs appeared. Then two long, thin delicate legs. The neck, long and furry, eased out. The baby's head, already squeaking pitifully, seemed too big for the skinny neck. The wet cria lay squirming on the grass. Its body was already covered with short, soft white fur. It's little nose and mouth were the color of ripe peaches. LuluBell called out, "Here I go, betcha mine is bigger than yours." And the second baby was quickly deposited on soft grass. Furbanks sniffed, "I'll just show these females. This is MY pasture and they don't even LIVE here! "I'm last, but my cria will be the most beautiful, watch this." And a perfect sixteen pound male cria entered the world. His short, curly black fur was still wet as Furbanks nudged him and he suckled almost at once.

Lynn Halybut knocked on the door, then pushed it open. Homer awakened quickly from his happy dream. "Homer, still in bed! Going to sleep all day? Have you forgotten this is a big day for us? We have much to do before everyone gets here."

"Oh, Mom, I just had the most wonderful dream. Just as the sun went down, the pregnant alpacas had perfect crias – one right after another. They wobbled a little then nursed right away." "In your dreams, my dear. You've been around alpacas since you were not much bigger than a new cria. Remember when you were so small we put you on an alpaca's back as if it were a pony? As you know, births are not always so easy. Now get up, please. Your dad needs help with the animals."

Reluctantly, Homer let go of his dream. Washing his face with cold water, he shoved his wet hands through rusty-red hair, kept short to avoid curls his mother admired. He threw extra icy splashes on his half closed eyes, blue as glacier ice and rimmed with straw-colored lashes. Quickly he pulled on old jeans and favorite ancient sweater. Lynn's knitting from their first alpaca years ago had gotten out of hand - it was huge. His baseball cap boosted "ALASKApacas." No need for rain gear, laid out the night before.

CHAPTER 2

Alaska's climate could be tricky. Today's forecast was a soaring forty degrees. But not long ago it had been minus twenty degrees Fahrenheit. Nearby the huge lake became a frozen shortcut for automobiles. Their criss-cross tracks across the snow reminded Homer of children in summer skipping rope Double Dutch. The neighbors' Great Pyrenees, padded easily across the ice on their big white feet to visit the Halybuts' ALASKApaca Ranch. Rocky and Lily, although friendly, frightened away strange dogs and troublesome critters with alpacas in mind. Lily was especially gentle. Each time she visited the neighbors she "borrowed" one of their chickens, tenderly carrying it home in her mouth like a kitten. The kidnapped chickens were returned and Lily was given her own rooster and a hen which laid a single egg each day.

Greg was already in the pasture. "Hi, son, I can use some help getting these male yearlings into the holding area." Homer, rattling the grain can, shouted "Come and get it. Hey, Buster, here's your morning treat. And bring your pals." A slight rattle of the grain can and alpacas across the pasture stopped grazing on grass. They like to be together and quickly surrounded him. Buster, self-appointed leader, had never met a handout he didn't like. Efficient as a vacuum cleaner, he gobbled grain. Homer pushed him away, "You're to share, Buster, don't be so greedy." Then the other males shyly shoved their muzzles into Homer's outstretched hand.

"Son, that's enough grain, you've got their attention. Now get behind them, spread out your arms. Make yourself look bigger. I'd like to get all these youngsters done while Charlie is here."

A truck pulled into the parking area. Tony and Alice, new alpaca owners came to help and learn. Alpacas often cost many thousands of dollars and first-time owners must learn much about their valuable animals. With good

care alpacas can live some twenty to twenty-five years. The new "parents" ensured that their two young females, Junebug and LuluBell, would become first-time mothers without complications. Lynn and Greg agreed to care for them until the birth of their babies. Then the dams and crias would travel many miles to their permanent home.

Alice and Tony watched a few minutes and learned where to be helpful and when to stay out of the way. They knew that neither alpacas nor llamas deserve their reputation of spitting on humans. The dominant animal will sometimes spit on a rival over dominance or food. So a smart human will stay out of their way.

When Greg was ready they herded a few alpacas at a time into the holding pen.

CHAPTER 3

A big black truck parked in the driveway. Charlie, star performer of the day, leaped out. His grin was as wide as his homeland – Australia. Sheep are much easier to shear than alpacas or llamas. Still he returned to the same ranches each year when the weather was beautiful. Then alpacas, sheared of their thick, warm coats, would not be stressed. The ranchers appreciated his work and pooled funds for the annual shearing at the Halybuts' ALASKApacas Ranch. Charlie enjoyed his work. The money was good, paid when he finished the job. Besides, Lynn's gracious hospitality was well known. Coffee, strong and hot, was always available. And her cinnamon rolls were irresistible.

Over six feet, about age thirty-five, Charlie was a working muscle mass. His broad chest seemed about to bust right through the skimpy black, sleeveless T-shirt. His arm muscles were huge and powerful. No nonsense black jeans seemed bonded to small hips and long, strong legs.

Homer envied Charlie and thought, "What a great job! He gets to travel, is <u>paid</u> to work with beautiful animals. And it keeps him in pretty good shape – for an older guy. Maybe I should become a sheep shearer."

Greg, yelling over the fence, interrupted Homer's shy admiration. "Homer, stop daydreaming! Bring three male yearlings into the holding pen. And I'll take one into the barn now." Three alpacas came right along, hoping for grain treats. Then Homer trotted Doodles from the holding pen into the barn.

Greg led the yearling onto the clean canvas-covered floor. Doodles was disappointed. "No grain! Why am I in this huge barn?" Doodles strongly resisted being forced to lie on his left side. Two men held down his furry front legs – two more men on his back legs. Another man held his neck and head off the floor. Doodles was without a care in the world. His Halybut family cared for him so well because they loved him. He didn't know they also valued his extremely fine coat of alpaca fiber. And, when he was two years old, he would sire beautiful babies. Suddenly Doodles was helpless and paralyzed with fear. "This huge man bending over my body is going to kill me with that black thing he's holding. And all these strangers are waiting to see a dead animal. Did I do a bad thing? Maybe I do spit at Buster, greediest male in my pasture. But I never spit on humans. Why is everybody mad at me?!"

Charlie's big h-u-u-u-m-m-m-i-n-g electric razor plunged into soft, white fur. Doodles was terrified! Charlie quickly sheared a tiny area from Doodles's right side, not far from the backbone. Calling out "SAMPLE!" he threw it as forcibly as you could throw a small cotton ball to the edge of the canvas. Lynn ran quickly, grabbing the fluffy fur before it got mixed up with other sheared wool. She stuffed it into a small plastic sandwich bag. Already written on the bag, "Doodles, male, twelve months, shearing date, ALASKApacas Ranch." This sample patch of wool, about as big as a chocolate bar, was very important..

Doodles couldn't struggle with all these men holding him. "Going to die anyway. I give up." Charlie sheared quickly. The men had relaxed their firm hold and were standing up. Doodles suddenly realized, "I'm FREE!" He dashed out the open barn door. The air was cool on his shorn body and the new short coat looked like thick corduroy. His pals, still in full coat, asked, "Where have you been? Why do you look so funny?" Eagerly he told them of his near-death experience, elaborating just a bit about how brave he had been.

The tiny first wool sample sheared from each alpaca is eagerly grabbed by the animal's owner. It is sent to a laboratory far away in Colorado where precise instruments measure how thick or fine the fiber is in microns. The smaller the microns, the more valuable it is. The very finest is called "Baby Alpaca."

Charlie worked quickly. About lunch time he was almost finished. Between animals he straightened up from the tiring position. Every six or so animals he sharpened the big razor. The barn was now dusty and Charlie put a mask over his nose and mouth. He wasn't much of a talker anyway. Furbanks, LuluBell and Junebug had been sheared with special care so that in their delicate condition they weren't too stressed. Soon the last animal frisked out of the barn and shearing was over for another year.

Large plastic bags of sheared alpaca waited for their owners to take home. Written on each bag was the animal's name and grade of wool. "Baby" usually comes from a cria but can also be from a mature alpaca. "Prime" is from side and back areas, called blanket and saddle. "Second" and "Third" cuts are neck and leg wool. Alpacas are usually sheared every two years and yield about four to six pounds of fiber.

A long, long time ago this wonderful fiber could only be worn by nobility, forbidden for ordinary people. But that's all changed. Now folks who spin, knit and weave eagerly buy lots of this warm, silky fiber. Alpacas come in more natural colors than any other animal so they have many lovely colors to choose from.

Charlie appreciated the profuse thanks and a combined check from grateful ranchers. Politely he declined the lunch for everyone which Lynn had already set out on the long picnic table. Tired but pleased that another shearing had gone well, he climbed into his truck. Smiling broadly, he waved, "Thanks everyone – see you next year." And lickety-split Charlie was down the road to his next job.

CHAPTER 4

Months passed. LuluBell and Junebug gave birth to females within a few days of each other. Furbanks's troublesome birthing took longer. Lynn, worried and anxious, said to herself, "Should I try to help or leave them alone?" She spoke lovingly to her beautiful alpaca, "Sweetheart, how I wish I could help you!" She stayed close by, watched intently, the veterinarian's phone number running through her mind, just in case. After much longer than most birthings, Furbanks's male cria entered the world. Exhausted, the new mother lay on the grass near her squeaking, well developed baby. Lynn quickly cleared mucus from the cria's mouth and toweled him off. Furbanks struggled to her feet. Gazing at her unsteady, hungry cria, she nuzzled him toward lunch and he guzzled greedily.

Every afternoon after school Homer ran straight to the maternity pasture. He was happy the birthing was over, but sorry he had missed his favorite's first-born. "Mom," Homer said seriously, "I'm saving the money you and Dad pay me for working on the ranch. First I'll go to college and study animal husbandry, or maybe veterinary medicine. After graduation I'll get a job and save enough money to buy my own alpaca." From his six foot height he looked down shyly at Lynn, "Maybe you'll sell me one at a discount?" Lynn was touched by his serious, well thought out future plans. She smiled at Homer's earnest enthusiasm. "Well, my dear, I'm sure your dad and I can work out something when the time comes."

"We haven't weighed Furbanks's cria yet. Would you like to do it?" Trembling with excitement, Homer gently and c-a-r-e-f-u-l-l-y cradled the silky black baby in his arms. "WOOO!! He weighs twenty pounds. How about naming him Moorage?" And Moorage it was.

Moorage, like most alpacas, enjoyed being close to his alpaca pals. But unlike many alpacas who are very shy, he welcomed grain treats from any human hand and allowed gentle strokes on his black, furry neck. His topknot had already grown over his big black eyes. Furbanks had weaned him at six months simply by walking away. Moorage quickly got the message, "This diner is now closed." He enthusiastically ate alpaca chow, hay and never turned down grain. The Halybuts agreed – Moorage would become a perfect public relations alpaca.

Saturday was Homer's sixteenth birthday, but there's never a holiday from animal and ranch chores. As he was chopping wild thistles out of a pasture, Greg and Lynn called to him from the gate. "Homer, please get Furbanks and Moorage into their halters and bring them here." Surprised at this unusual request, Homer lead his favorite friends to his waiting parents. He handed Furbanks's blue lead to Greg. Lynn took the young alpaca's red lead. Lynn smiled happily and Greg looked a little less serious than usual. Homer thought, "What's up? They've never acted like this before."

Lynn bubbled with enthusiasm. "Homer, we've had to keep our secret for a long time. Today is your sixteenth birthday and we have presents for you. She handed him Furbanks's lead as Greg gave him Moorage's. "Furbanks and Moorage now belong to you! HAPPY BIRTHDAY!" Homer, speechless, accepted the leads, his eyes spilling over with tears. He could only squeak, "Thank you, thank you." His mother kissed his wet cheek and his father shook his hand, man to man, then hugged him. That night Homer was so excited he couldn't sleep for the longest time. He kept saying to himself, "My own alpacas. I still can't believe it!"

CHAPTER 5

Alaska's annual State Fair was a big event for the Matanuska Valley. Farmers are known the world over for the heroic size of their vegetables, fruits and beautiful flowers. Competition is keen for the biggest and best in each category. Countless rainbow-colored banners flap gaily announcing this much anticipated event. The huge exhibition halls temporarily house animals great and small. The Halybuts were not farmers but they enjoyed showing their alpacas. Alpaca people practice many hours with their animals in fiercely competitive routines. Contestants hope to win generous cash prizes donated by local merchants and winning animals proudly wear blue or red ribbons for first or second place. Pink, green, white and yellow ribbons prove they are also winners.

A short summer season with day and night sunlight makes crops grow very quickly and valley farmers' vegetables and fruits grow to enormous size. Imagine tennis ball sized radishes and ninety pound cabbages!

Proud of Furbanks and Moorage, Homer planned to enter them in the Alpaca Dam and Cria Contest. Furbanks's first wool sample was "Baby," the finest quality. Moorage's jet black coat was especially handsome and he was not skittish nor shy among humans. Homer was confident they would show well in public.

Every day after school they practiced commands. Some trainers prefer the word "behavior." Commands or behaviors are instructions to animals so that each understands the other. Animals learn to obey without fuss. Some commands are: follow calmly on a lead, stand, kush (kneel down), and present foot for inspection.

Homer set up a simple obstacle course in the pasture of old tires laid on the ground in rows. Furbanks went around several tires instead of stepping

through them. "No, Furbanks, that's cheating. Go back and do it again, like this." And he showed her once more. Soon she played the game correctly and Homer gave her a small grain treat.

Homer constructed simple low hurdles, raising them as they became too easy for Furbanks. At a challenging height she went UNDER them. "No, Furbanks, you must go OVER every hurdle. You could jump much higher than these if you really wanted to. Remember when the moose wandered near your pasture? He was huge and hungry with a face only another moose could love. You were so scared you jumped the pasture fence. Then you were on the same side as the moose! He could have stomped you to death but he wasn't interested in you. He just wanted fresh buds and leaves. So pretend I'm a moose and JUMP!" Furbanks tried again. "Good girl! You went over that hurdle, graceful as a gazelle. Gazelles are small, swift African animals, but they're not as furry and beautiful as you." Moorage wanted to play, but he was too young and small. The winning owners receive cash prizes. Winning animals proudly wear on their harnesses a ribbon of gold, blue, red or white. "Next year, Moorage, you can play too."

CHAPTER 6

The big day came swiftly. Lynn fed Max and Reggie early, the food quickly and noisily slurped up. They pleaded, "Hey, is that all we get?" Greg was preparing the truck for its five passengers and all the stuff necessary at the fair. Many trips to the barn for water bucket, hay, grain, broom and shovel. Last but very important was the can of alpaca starter "beans." Alpacas are so clean they all "go" in the same pile, once given the idea. And they are polite. This sample of familiar dung is poured onto the ground in an out-of-the-way location. The dominant alpaca is first to back over the potty pile while the lower rank wait patiently in line. Clean up is quick and easy.

Greg and Lynn watched, ready to help Homer load his alpacas into the horse trailer. Furbanks remembered riding in the trailer once before so she hopped right in. Moorage wasn't sure he wanted to enter that dark, small area. Homer encouraged him by lifting his front legs onto the edge of the trailer, then a forceful shove on his back side. Moorage quickly decided this was the place to be. Mom, already kushed, was quietly chomping hay. With Lynn and Homer up front, Greg eased out of the driveway with his precious cargo.

The animal exhibition hall was huge and brightly lighted. They quickly found their small, temporary corral. A lettered sign read:

<u>HALYBUT - ALASKApacas Ranch</u>
   Breed: **Huacaya Alpaca**
   Dam: **Furbanks Age: 3 1/2 years**
   Cria: **Moorage Age: 7 months**

Homer filled the water bucket, setting it in a corner on the dirt floor. The round hole of the hay sack bulged with luscious leafy hay as he hung it onto the corral bars. Then he offered a handful of grain to comfort his animals in their new, temporary home.

The hall was abuzz with people getting their animals settled in. Lynn and Greg walked around looking at alpacas, other animals being exhibited and spectacular vegetables, fruits and flowers. Soon they were back and Greg had that look on his face. "I know, Dad, chores waiting to be done on the ranch. I'm ready, let's go." Homer kissed their topknots and assured his alpacas, "I'll be back to see you EVERY DAY. If you're good I'll bring you treats."

CHAPTER 7

Moorage kushed in the dark beside Furbanks who slept peacefully. He couldn't sleep in this strange, new place and gently nuzzled her warm, fawn colored coat. Still she slept. Like dogs' paws, alpacas have padding under their small, two-toed feet. His tiny toenails made only faint clicking sounds as he stood up. Scratching his itchy, furry topknot vigorously on the metal bars, the corral door opened slowly, silently. He looked around. "WOW! Lots of strange animals are here. I've never been anywhere alone. I'll walk around a little. Be back before Mom wakes up and fusses at me for leaving."

He walked slowly down the isle. "Hey, over here, little buddy. You lost? You sure are a cute baby llama. Don't go too far from your mom. You're not even weaned."

Moorage stood up straight trying to look as big as possible. Although he stretched, his head only reached a tad above the llama's knees. He thought, "Furbanks told me about the camelid family and how we are related. I didn't understand a word of it. But I know this big muzzle guzzling hay belongs to a llama. Long pieces of hay stick out and bounce up and down as he chews from side to side. He looks so funny! What big yellow teeth he has. His eyes are black like Mom's with even longer eyelashes."

"Nice of you to ask, Mr. Llama. I'm not lost – YET anyway. I'm a seven months old alpaca, almost fully grown. And I CERTAINLY don't suckle any more! My mother, Furbanks, is a beautiful huacaya (wa-ka-ya) breed. She came from Peru and I'm her first cria. Biggest place I've ever seen. Bye, see you later."

Fascinated by so many animals, Moorage walked on. "Hi, Mrs. Pig. What squirmy, pink babies you're feeding. Do you like grain? It's my favorite food,

except for fresh carrots." "Hello, little llama. You should eat lots of grain to grow bigger." "Mam, I'm not a llama. I'm actually big for my age. Alpacas are different from llamas when you get to know us. So long, Mrs. Pig. I'd like to stay and talk but there's so much to see."

A short, fat creature waddled past. Its feathers changed colors like bubbles in sunlight. Soft gray to shiny, reddish color, then to glossy black. "Morning, Mrs. Duck. What pretty fuzzy little duckies are following you. Will they grow up to be gooses like you?" "Thank you, llama cria. Yes, they are pretty and I'm proud of them. I'm an Egyptian goose, a rare breed actually. My goslings are fluffy now. But in a month or so they will look like me. I must tell you the plural (more than one) of goose is GEESE. Ducks are ducks and more than one goose is geese." "Thanks, Mrs. Goose, I'll remember that. Now I must correct you. Llamas and alpacas are different. I'm a huacaya alpaca with straight wool. Suri (sir-ee) alpacas have silkier wool which parts over the back-bone and hangs down in long curls. Fully grown I'll weigh about 165 pounds. See my ears? They're pointy. Llama ears are banana shaped. Alpaca wool is dense and fine and we come in more colors than any other wool producing animal. Nice talking with you, Mrs. Goose. I must tell more animals about alpacas."

He hurried past huge cows with scary horns longer than his short legs. Horses with beautiful golden manes and tails stood patiently. Their feet were bigger around than a catcher's mitt. If he got in their way they could squuuush him like a bug.

He came to a cluster of small white fur pillowcases set on short legs. A black pillowcase strolled over, "Hello, baby llama. You aren't much bigger than we are. How old are you? We are Toy Cheviot, a very special breed of sheep. So few of us remain in the world, only about one hundred, we are ENDANGERED. That means after the Toy Cheviot sheep alive now are gone there will be no more." Moorage was shocked and horrified that such a terrible thing could happen to beautiful animals. He said "I'm so sorry to learn you are endangered. Makes me sad to think about it."

"I'm a huacaya breed of alpaca. Suri alpacas have silky, long curls. Huacayas have fluffy coats and often the locks of fiber have little ridge-like waves. Both breeds are different from llamas, and there are lots more llamas here than alpacas. Our parents, called "umbria" (dams) and "macho" (sires), came from far away South America where there are a great many alpacas. As soon as they got to the United States our parents were put in quarantine for months, away from all other animals. Americans were not being mean, they were making sure the alpacas didn't have diseases which could spread to other animals. Since there are so few Toy Cheviot sheep please HURRY! Make lots of pretty sheep babies."

Moorage was curious about unusual things, especially new food treats. He hummed to himself, "Wonder what those long orange shapes are at the end of this aisle?" Walking faster, he could hardly believe his eyes. "These are orange baseball bats. But they smell like CARROTS - my favorite treats. Well, actually ONE of my favorite treats. Matanuska Valley folks boast about the size of their fruits and veggies. But these can't be real carrots. Maybe I should just bite one and see." And he did. "DELICIOUS! But I'm sure ALL of them couldn't be that good." He bit into another, mumbling with his mouth full. "Yep, very tasty! What nice humans to bring these fresh free treats. I must tell all the animals after I taste one more carrot. I do get tired of hay every day but NEVER refuse grain – or hay either, now that I think about it." Soon just one carrot remained – with a big bite out of it.

CHAPTER 8

He walked past cabbages too big to fit into a kitchen sink. Zucchini as long as his body. Radishes bigger than a child's fist. Humming right along, Moorage exclaimed, "Something smells delicious! Wow! – fresh fruit. What a feast – red raspberries, blackberries, blueberries and red currants. Such big bunches of grapes. Strawberries so big and fat only twelve fill an egg carton. I didn't know apples came in red, green and yellow. Each one is like a jewel set in colored tissue paper."

His short, furry legs were stretched to the limit. "One more step over these onions and I can reach an apple. Never really liked onions. They just don't smell nice. But the purple ones are pretty and almost as big as volley balls. Oops, just upset the whole box." Purple, brown and white onions rolled down the isle toward Mrs. Pig. "Hopes she likes onions."

Reaching for a green apple, Moorage accidentally stepped right into the middle of the box. Apples rolled merrily down the aisle, playing a game with onions – which could roll fastest and farthest down the isle? Pierced by sharp alpaca toes, festive tissue paper stuck to Moorage's short, furry legs. The more he fidgeted to get rid of the paper, the tighter it clung to his fuzzy legs. He looked so silly, like a clumsy clown. The wispy paper tickled his nose. Sneezing violently, pink, purple and green tissue papers flew up in all directions, floating down like dizzy butterflies.

Suddenly Moorage remembered Furbanks. "How long have I been exploring? Mom must be awake by now. I'd better hurry back so she can fuss at me." Turning down a wide isle, he muttered to no one in particular, "All aisles look the same. I'm LOST!"

CHAPTER 9

High above his head a loud, whiny voice complained. "Moorage, why are you outside your corral? Your mother is frantic. Wait 'til she sees the greedy mess you've made. The farmers will kill you for what you've done to their prize exhibits." Anxious and frightened, Moorage hummed nervously to himself. A different kind of huuuuumm than when he talked to his alpaca buddies. He had never felt so small and scared.

S-T-R-E-T-C-H-I-N-G his slender neck upward, as far as it would go, he saw four skinny, long brown legs. Above the huge knobby knees, brown hair, long and rough, covered a chest as tall and wide as the Halybut's truck.

The monster's booming voice echoed throughout the big building. "I am Kaffir Kamel, largest of the camelid family." Intending to educate young Moorage, he continued. "I weigh twenty-six times more than you, little alpaca. Camelids include llamas (YAM-MUZ), which are related to the guanaco (WHAH-KNOCK-O). A closer relative to you, Moorage, is the smaller graceful vicuna (vye-COON-yuh). Humans shear us camelids in warm weather. Shearing keeps us cool and doesn't hurt. The hair grows right back before winter. Our sheared fiber is spun into soft, strong yarn for beautiful, warm garments."

"We are often confused with the Dromedary camel with one hump. My head is similar to yours, but much larger. No one ever mistakes me for a llama or says I'm cute."

Kaffir had more to teach this inquisitive youngster. "Back up, Moorage, so you can see me. These two large humps on my back tell you I'm a Bactrian camel. Two humps, like the letter 'B' Get it, TWO humps?!"

Plaintively Moorage said, "Mr. Kamel, will you please help me? I was having such a good time but now I'm lost. I want to find my mom. You're so tall, can you see Furbanks? Please tell her I'm with you."

Kaffir, huge and powerful, remembered long ago when he was a young calf, lost in the desert. "Moorage, you are young, intelligent and curious and have learned a lesson today. I will help you."

Kaffir bellowed his most outraged bawl. "Furbanks – your cria is with me." Every animal in the huge room shuddered. Furbanks came running. "Moorage, I've been so worried. Are you alright?" Relieved to find her wandering cria, she forgot to scold him. Humming happily, he nuzzled her soft coat. "But," he thought, "how will I explain all those treats I ate?" "Mom," he whined, "will the farmers really kill me, like Mr. Kamel said?"

Suddenly electric lights blazed high overhead. Moorage thought, "A great adventure makes time go fast. Must be morning already." Furbanks stood still, her ears laid back. "I don't remember the way to our corral." Suddenly, her ears alert, she heard a familiar voice. "What a surprise to find YOU here! I thought I had locked the corral gate last night. Hope you weren't scared in this huge building. Let's go this way." Homer's alpacas were so happy to see him they didn't beg for treats.

Following Homer down the wide aisle, Furbanks was uneasy. The thick mop of her fawn colored topknot covered her shiny black eyes. But she could see perfectly well. "Who is this person whose voice is just like Homer's?"

Quietly she hummed to Moorage. "This human is very different from our Homer. He even SMELLS different. If this is the teenager who cares for us, where are the old, raggedy, faded blue pants and floppy sweater?" Moorage, sharing her fear, shyly backed away from this handsome stranger. Furbanks hummed again. "This young man is wearing black pants which fit just right. A black, stringy thing, like a shoelace with silver ends, ties the neck of his spotless white shirt. And his black vest has silver buttons! Can't be Homer." Understanding their cautious concern, Homer returned his animals to their corral.

His parents had taken Homer to the festival many times but this was his first time as a participant. It was important that his animals feel confident and happy, although HE was nervous and scared. Putting his arms around Furbanks's neck, he hugged her gently, and kissed her topknot. Then he stroked the black, soft wool of Moorage's slender neck while speaking to him quietly. "I'll be right back. I have to get our number for the alpaca events." Furbanks, reassured, whispered to her cria, "It is our Homer. He's all grown up."

Homer returned wearing **NUMBER 12** on a big white card which covered his chest. He sighed, "The event I'm really interested in is the ALPACA DAM and CRIA category. BUMMER! It's the last event of alpaca competitions and we will be the last contestants to be judged."

CHAPTER 10

Inside the enormous building seats filled up fast around the show ring. In a festival mood, folks balanced food, special to all fairs, on flimsy paper plates. Topped with onions, relish, catsup and mustard, hot dogs and hamburgers were slurped and burped along with trendy drinks. Big brass belt buckles got tighter over round bellies. Kids gnawed on apples impaled on sticks, solidly encased in tooth-bustin' red sugar coating.

Competitive alpaca games were about to begin. Animals and handlers in colorful, imaginative costumes brought cheers and laughter from the crowd. Homer, in his conservative black and white show attire, felt his stomach tighten. Handlers went through most obstacles with their animals. When an alpaca stopped still in the middle of the game, the handler coaxed and encouraged the animal to continue, success not guaranteed. Some of the games were similar to Homer's at the ranch. Circles lay flat on the straw-covered dirt floor, like big and small hoops. Alpacas jumped varying heights of hurdles, their handlers running alongside encouragingly. Narrow wooden bridges arching over shallow pools of water were too much for some timid alpacas. They wouldn't put a foot on them. Trellis-like frames dangling lengths of cloth, yarn and small soft objects looked scary to several alpacas. Pleading and encouragement were useless. They didn't have THAT much trust in their handlers to mess with this Halloweenish display. "Forget it. Treat or no treat I'm not going through there."

The obstacle course games were over and handlers accepted prizes and fancy ribbons. A large male alpaca, the winner last year, came in first again with a blue ribbon. Homer and Furbanks came in second. Pinning the red ribbon on her halter, Homer hugged and praised Furbanks. And he was very pleased with his crinkly new fifty dollar bill.

Games were fun and Homer was glad they had won a prize. But he longed to win the final alpaca contest:

BEST OF BREED: HUACAYA OR SURI, DAM & CRIA.

During his devoted care of Furbanks and Moorage he had often daydreamed of winning this most important event.

CHAPTER 11

A loudspeaker squeaked then made an announcement, interrupting the noisy babble of many people having a good time. "ATTENTION PLEASE! Attention please. Will the owner of the animals which escaped their corral last night please come to the office immediately." The message was so important it was repeated.

Astonished, Homer thought, "I was first through the entrance when they unlocked it this morning. How could anyone know I found Furbanks and Moorage wandering in the isle?" Puzzled and worried, he hurried to the office.

Two Fair officials awaited him. "Hello, Homer. I'm Fred Frakus and this is John Jummpup. We're sorry to tell you this, but one or both of your alpacas is in big trouble. The security guard made his rounds at five this morning before the building was open to the public. Of course we were at home then, but the call was recorded. Please listen to his report."

"This is Joe, Security. I made my usual security check at zero five hundred hours. I saw an animal acting very strangely near the fruits and vegetables exhibits. Looked like a young llama, fine black coat. Several displays had been overturned and fruits and vegetables had rolled all over the floor. The carrot display had been destroyed, only one large carrot was left – with a bite out of it. The animal's legs were covered in colored tissue paper and it seemed to be having some kind of seizure. I thought of calling one of our veterinarians as I watched the animal closely for a few minutes. Then I walked toward it but I've never seen anything move so fast. It was gone in the blink of an eye. I tried to find the animal but didn't see which way it went. And this is such a huge place. I walked to the llama and alpaca corrals and one gate was open. Sign said owner was HALYBUT of ALASKApacas Ranch. So I'm calling to report this incident. Joe, Security, signing out at zero five thirty."

Mr. Frakus continued. "We got here as soon as possible but the animal or animals had disappeared. We've been unable to learn more details. You are the only person answering our announcement and the only owner of a young black alpaca. So Moorage must be the culprit. We appreciate your coming forward. Please tell us what happened."

Homer was horrified at what Moorage seemed to have done. "I'm sure I locked my corral before leaving yesterday. But this morning the corral was empty and I found both Furbanks and Moorage lost and wandering in the aisle. I don't know what happened. But I take full responsibility. Please tell me what I must do."

Mr. Jummpup spoke sympathetically. "Well, Homer, we sympathize and appreciate your attitude, but the farmers are understandably upset and expect to be paid for their destroyed displays. Here is their list of complaints and amounts to be paid."

Sadly Homer walked back to his corral. He talked to his animals. "I wish I could hum like you do. It would make it easier for me to explain our problem. Furbanks, you are too shy and gentle to have gotten into trouble. Moorage, you're always curious about everything. You have lots of energy and are always hungry. These are good traits most of the time. But now we're in big trouble."

Lynn and Greg returned after looking at exhibits in this huge fair. Homer reluctantly told them of Moorage's exploring. Then he said, "I have to take these guys to the arena right now. Number twelve is about to be called and I can't keep the judges waiting. I'm in enough trouble already. I hope they haven't heard about mischievous Moorage."

CHAPTER 12

The contest was for **BEST OF BREED: HUACAYA OR SURI, DAM &
CRIA.** The event was already in progress and Homer and his huacayas were
the last entries. The judges, one woman and two men, must agree on the best
combination dam and her cria.

The lady judge, serious, gentle and polite, approached Homer. "May we
touch your dam and cria?" "Yes, please." Each judge calmly wrote notes as they
examined Furbanks and Moorage. They looked for best physical conformity of
chest, legs, back, eyes, quality of wool, response to commands, and over-all
behavior. The judges smiled, and left, "Thank you, Mr. Halybut." Homer and his
alpacas were tired – it had been a long day. And he had a lot to think about.

Homer's parents stayed at the corral. They knew if they watched the judging it would make him even more nervous than he was. Lynn shook her head
sadly, "Homer is only sixteen years old. Do you think we should have waited
until he is older to give him these superb, valuable alpacas?" "No, my dear.
Homer is a very responsible young man. He gives these animals excellent
loving care. I can't believe Homer would forget to lock the corral last night."
Lynn looked closely at the lock. "Greg, I think you should examine this lock.
It looks odd." Greg, puzzled, locked it, then pulled firmly. The lock opened at
once and the corral door could be opened with the slightest effort. "Lynn, you
try it." Same results. Greg was positive, "This lock is definitely defective. A
firm push by young Moorage would have opened the corral door. We must tell
the Fair officials. When Homer comes back it would be nice if you were here
to talk with him. He's really worried about Moorage's adventurous and destruc-
tive night. And the competition in the Dam and Cria Contest looks pretty keen.
I'm going to ask an official to come over and take a look at this lock."

Homer led his alpacas back to the corral. He knew that animals can't understand the changing ways of humans. But they know when something is different or troubling and often they react to the handler's mood. So when working with his animals Homer always tried to be happy and positive. Although he was too tired to even wonder how it would feel to win this contest, he praised Furbanks and Moorage for excellent behavior and promised them grain treats. Time passed slowly and still no announcement of winners in the Dam and Cria Contest. He wondered, "Why is it taking so long to announce the winners!"

CHAPTER 13

Suddenly the loudspeaker crackled and popped shushing the noisy crowd. "Will the following owners please bring their animals to the judging area." Homer listened hopefully for his name but instead he heard, "Miss Blah, Mr. Blah, Blah, blah, blah." Then the hum of the crowd resumed. The winning categories had been announced and his hopes sank like rocks in a pond. Uncomfortable in his show clothes, he longed to be back at the ranch in raggedy jeans and beat up sweater. "After all that work and so many hours, my alpacas didn't even place last!" Furbanks and Moorage knew him so well, Homer had to try really hard to hide his dark mood from them. They turned back toward the corral.

Once again the loudspeaker suddenly bellowed: **"ATTENTION, PLEASE! Mr. Homer Halybut, please bring your alpacas to the judging area."** Homer stopped still in the aisle, "What's going on! I think I just heard my name called. Naaa, couldn't be. Or maybe some one else is angry about Moorage's midnight feast." Then the loud, imperious voice again. **"The first place winner of the ALPACA DAM & CRIA contest goes to"** - (a looong pause) **"MR. HOMER HALYBUT and huayaca alpacas FURBANKS and MOORAGE of ALASKApacas Ranch!"**

Homer thought, "I'm frozen in a dream. I can't move." Again the loud voice: "HOMER! Please come and receive your winners' ribbons. And a check for five hundred dollars! You will also receive a year's supply of any grain your superb alpacas prefer. CONGRATULATIONS!"

The crowd cheered and applauded wildly. Homer, bewildered and still in a daze, led his alpacas to the lady judge. She handed him an over-sized check and shook his sweaty hand. She spoke with such enthusiasm her voice could be heard from Alaska to the lower 48 states "Homer, this is a great achievement! You are the youngest alpaca owner ever to win this prize." She handed him the microphone. "Would you like to say a few words to your friends?"

Homer had never spoken into a microphone and was so nervous his voice trembled with emotion. "I want to tell my parents how much I appreciate your trusting me with Furbanks and Moorage. And to the judges who awarded us this honor, thank you very much. To my young 4-H member friends I would like to donate one hundred dollars of this generous check to our group. Keep loving and caring for your animals. Thank you all!"

The contest was over at last. He had won!! Forgetting how tired he was, now he felt like a soaring balloon. Homer talked to his alpacas as they hurried back to the corral. "You were great, guys. Aren't you glad we practiced every day at the ranch! I've never been so happy. Well, yes, I have. On my sixteenth birthday when my folks gave you to me."

CHAPTER 14

Homer's joyful mood vanished when he remembered the farmers' complaints. He pulled the lengthy list from his pocket. "Wow! three hundred dollars. Moorage, your nighttime adventures were expensive. Couldn't you have snacked on something cheaper?" He sighed, "Maybe I shouldn't have promised 4-H a hundred dollars. This leaves me with only one hundred for my college fund. But it's too late now. A promise is a promise and they need help. I'll have to find another way to make money."

Lynn and Greg were thrilled at Homer's success and generosity. They surrounded him with a huge hug. Greg, never gushy with enthusiasm, "Homer, you did a great job! Furbanks, Moorage, how about a treat?" They gobbled the offered grain and kushed contentedly.

Homer wanted to get the bad part over with. "Dad I'll cash this check and send three hundred dollars to Mr. Frakus for the farmers. I don't blame them for being mad. I hope Moorage will be satisfied with our treats from now on."

"Son, I have good news for you. The officials examined the lock and agreed that it was broken. Moorage simply took advantage of the situation like a curious youngster. Fred Frakus told us that the fee we paid to participate in the Fair assured us of a secure corral. Since the lock was not secure, the Fair is assuming responsibility for what happened. So the Fair will reimburse the farmers."

Like sun breaking through clouds, Homer's face glowed with joy and relief. "What a WONDERFUL day this has been. Let's go home!" And they did.

Hurrying home the Halybuts relived the happy day. Cozily kushed while munching hay, Furbanks and Moorage couldn't wait to tell their alpaca pals about their amazing adventure.